DANGEROUS ADVENTURES

Sailing Adventures

by Anne M. Todd

CAPSTONE
HIGH-INTEREST
BOOKS

an imprint of Capstone Press
Mankato, Minnesota

Capstone High-Interest Books are published by Capstone Press
151 Good Counsel Drive, P.O. Box 669, Mankato, Minnesota 56002
http://www.capstone-press.com

Library of Congress Cataloging-in-Publication Data
Todd, Anne.
   Sailing adventures/by Anne M. Todd.
   p. cm.—(Dangerous adventures)
   Includes bibliographical references and index.
   ISBN 0-7368-0906-6
   1. Sailing—Juvenile literature. [1. Sailing.] I. Title. II. Series.
GV811.13 .T63 2002
797.1'24—dc21   00-013091

Summary: Describes adventures in sailing, including a description of how sailboats
work, equipment sailors use, historic sailing expeditions, and recent sailing adventures.

Editorial Credits
Tom Adamson, editor; Lois Wallentine, product planning editor; Heather Kindseth,
   cover designer; Timothy Halldin, production designer; Katy Kudela,
   photo researcher

Photo Credits
Archive Photos, 12, 14, 18, 20
Bettmann/CORBIS, 28
Billy Black, cover, 4, 6, 8, 10, 36, 44
Camera Press Ltd./Archive Photos, 34
FPG International LLC, 32
Francois Mousis/http://mousis.free.fr, 38, 40
New Bedford Whaling Museum, 22, 26

Capstone High-Interest Books thanks Nim Marsh, Associate Editor at
Cruising World **magazine, for helping to prepare this book.**

1 2 3 4 5 6 07 06 05 04 03 02

117 -5946

Table of Contents

Chapter 1

Sailing

On July 22, 1996, Subaru Takahashi set sail from Tokyo, Japan. He planned to sail alone across the Pacific Ocean on a 30-foot (9-meter) boat. Takahashi had packed navigation and radio equipment, food, and water. He expected the trip to take two months.

Takahashi soon faced serious problems. An engine on the boat quit and caused a power failure. For five weeks, he had no lights, no automatic steering, and no global positioning system (GPS). Without this device, he had no easy way to know where he was on the ocean.

Takahashi's radio battery died five days after the power failure. He lost all communication with people on land. He could not talk to

Some sailors attempt to sail alone around the world.

Sailors use ropes to adjust the sails.

anyone or get weather information for the rest of his journey across the Pacific. Yet he arrived safely in San Francisco on September 13. The trip covered about 6,000 miles (9,650 kilometers).

Takahashi's accomplishment set a new record. He was the youngest person to sail solo across the Pacific Ocean. Takahashi was only 14 years old.

Expeditions

Sailors sometimes go on expeditions. These long journeys can last a few months or as long as several years. Sailors sometimes are members of expedition teams. Other sailors choose to go on an expedition alone.

Sailors go on expeditions for a variety of reasons. In the past, people sailed to discover new lands and to find new trade routes. They sailed to prove that Earth was round. They sailed to make detailed maps of unexplored areas.

Today, most sailors sail for fun. Other people sail to break records. They may try to make the fastest trip across an ocean. Some sailors try to sail around the world alone in the fastest time.

Sailboats

Sailboats have one or more sails. Ropes attach the sails to a pole called a mast. Wind pushes against the sails to move the boat. Sailors steer the boat by turning a rudder.

Sailboats can move easily in the same direction that the wind is blowing. Sailors cannot sail directly into the wind. They sail

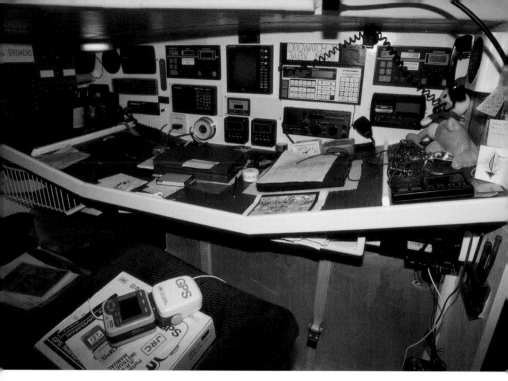

Sailors today use modern equipment such as radios and global positioning systems.

in a zigzag pattern to move the boat forward. This technique is called tacking.

Sailboats are classified according to the number and position of their masts and sails. There are several different types of sailboats. Two of these are sloops and ketches. Sloops are the most simply designed sailboats. They have one mast. A mainsail is attached to the back of the mast. A headsail is attached to the front of the mast. Ketches have two masts. A shorter mast is located behind the taller mast.

Equipment

Early explorers found their position at sea in a variety of ways. They sometimes navigated by the North Star. This star always is to the north. They also used compasses. A compass contains a magnetized needle that points north.

By the 1700s, sailors used sextants to find their location at sea. These devices measure the angle of the sun from the horizon. Sailors use this angle to figure out their latitude. Latitude is the distance north or south of the equator.

Today, sailors use more advanced equipment to find their location. GPS devices receive signals from satellites that orbit Earth. Sailors determine their exact position with these signals.

Sailors also use communication systems that were not available in the past. Boats have radios that allow sailors to call other boats at sea or to get weather reports. Some boats have computers

Sailors wear rain gear to protect themselves from rain and spray from high waves.

or fax machines. Sailors can e-mail or fax while at sea.

Sailors also need safety equipment on board. Life jackets can save sailors from drowning if they fall into the water. Sailors wear several layers of clothing. They can add or remove clothes depending on the weather. A waterproof jacket protects sailors from rain and spray from high waves. Some sailors wear gloves to protect their hands from the ropes and from cold weather.

Sailors also should carry an emergency kit. This kit might include a knife, tape, signal flares, a flashlight, a first aid kit, binoculars, and extra rope. The kit also should include extra food and water. The emergency kit should be kept in a waterproof bag.

Sailing Dangers

Sailors face many dangers. Bad weather can be deadly. Strong winds and large waves can cause boats to stray from their course. Sailors can become lost. Strong winds also can cause boats to capsize. Capsized boats are flipped over in the water. Sailors check the boat's equipment carefully before setting sail. They make sure the equipment will work in an emergency.

Sailors protect themselves from sunburn. The sun's rays reflect off the water. Ultraviolet (UV) rays from the sun can damage the skin and eyes. Sailors wear sunscreen to prevent sunburn. They wear sunglasses with UV protection and hats to protect their eyes and faces.

Chapter 2

Early Explorers

In 1522, a group of sailors became the first people to successfully circumnavigate the world. These sailors were the first crew to sail completely around the world.

Ferdinand Magellan

Ferdinand Magellan's crew is credited with being the first to circumnavigate the world. The trip's purpose was to find a western route from Europe to the Spice Islands. This group of islands is located off the southeastern coast of Asia. Today, these islands are part of Indonesia.

On September 20, 1519, Magellan and about 250 sailors set sail from Spain. The crew

Ferdinand Magellan led the first crew to circumnavigate the world.

Magellan was killed in the Philippine Islands during a battle.

sailed on five ships. Each ship carried weapons and enough food to last two years.

The crew stopped in Rio de Janeiro in South America. The men repaired the ships and brought more food aboard.

Many of the sailors became sick during the first part of their journey. They suffered from a disease called scurvy. A lack of vitamin C causes this disease. This vitamin is found in many fruits, including oranges and tomatoes. But the sailors did not know this. They had brought no fruit on board. In Rio de Janeiro, the crew ate plenty of fruit. The effects of scurvy disappeared after they ate this fruit. For the time, they were cured.

The Strait of Magellan

Magellan's crew continued south along the coast of South America. They eventually discovered a strait near the southern tip of South America. A strait is a narrow strip of water that connects two larger bodies of water.

Magellan sent one ship called the *San Antonio* to explore the strait. Magellan and the others waited for the *San Antonio* to return. They waited for a week. Finally, Magellan sent a search team to locate the ship. They could not find it. The captain of the *San Antonio* had returned to Spain.

The remaining ships sailed through the strait. The strait later was named the Strait of Magellan. Magellan's crew members found a huge body of water when they reached the

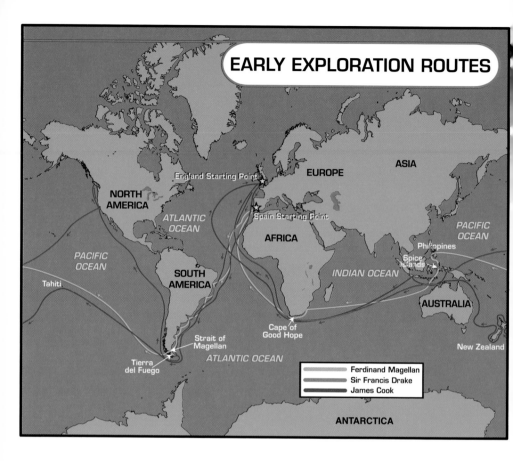

EARLY EXPLORATION ROUTES

England Starting Point
EUROPE
ASIA
NORTH AMERICA
ATLANTIC OCEAN
Spain Starting Point
AFRICA
PACIFIC OCEAN
PACIFIC OCEAN
Philippines
Spice Islands
Tahiti
SOUTH AMERICA
INDIAN OCEAN
AUSTRALIA
Cape of Good Hope
Strait of Magellan
New Zealand
Tierra del Fuego
ATLANTIC OCEAN

Ferdinand Magellan
Sir Francis Drake
James Cook

ANTARCTICA

other side. They thought the Spice Islands and Asia had to be near. But the Pacific Ocean is much wider than the crew thought.

The Pacific Ocean
Many of the crew members became sick soon after sailing onto the Pacific Ocean. The food had gone bad. Meat and biscuits contained

worms. The water was unfit to drink. Some sailors died. The conditions soon became worse. The food ran out. Some sailors ate rats and sawdust. They even tried to eat leather. They soaked it in water for a few days to soften it.

At last, the weak sailors saw land. They arrived at the Philippine Islands. Magellan explored the islands and met the people who lived there. Magellan wanted to take control of an island called Mactan. He led an army of soldiers to fight the natives. On April 27, 1521, Magellan died during the battle on Mactan.

Juan Sebastián de Elcano then took command of the crew. Only 17 other sailors and one ship remained. They sailed across the Indian Ocean and around the Cape of Good Hope. They then sailed up the western coast of Africa. In September 1522, the ship returned to Spain.

Magellan's crew had found a western route to the Spice Islands. They also had sailed around the world.

Sir Francis Drake led the second voyage to circumnavigate the world.

Sir Francis Drake

On December 13, 1577, Sir Francis Drake set sail from England. He sailed with a fleet of five ships and almost 200 sailors. They planned to sail through the Strait of Magellan. They would then attack Spanish settlements on the western coast of South America. Drake took valuable goods from other ships he met during his travels.

The ships ran into severe weather when they reached the Strait of Magellan. They sailed around Cape Horn instead of going through the stormy strait. Drake's ship was called the *Golden Hind.* This ship became separated from the others. The other ships then turned around and sailed back to England. The *Golden Hind* continued alone.

Drake and his crew became the first people from England to cross the Pacific Ocean. Once across, Drake traded goods in the Spice Islands. He packed more goods onto the already full ship. This extra weight made the ship sit lower in the water. As the ship left, it became stuck on a reef. These dangerous rocky areas are near the water's surface. Drake threw cannons and other weapons overboard to lighten the ship. The *Golden Hind* escaped only after a change in wind direction.

In September 1580, Drake and his crew arrived in England. Drake was treated as a hero. He had led the second ship to circumnavigate the world.

Englishman James Cook explored and mapped much of the Pacific Ocean.

James Cook

James Cook sailed from England on August 25, 1768. He sailed on a ship called the *Endeavour* with a crew of 94 sailors and scientists. They planned to explore new lands and make new detailed maps of the Pacific Ocean.

On April 13, 1769, Cook and his crew arrived at Tahiti. This island is in the South Pacific Ocean. They stayed there until July. Cook studied and mapped the area. He and an astronomer also observed a transit of Venus. They looked through a telescope as the planet Venus passed in front of the Sun. Transits of Venus are rare.

The crew then sailed to New Zealand and on to Australia. Cook was able to keep his crew free of scurvy. The ship's food supply included fruit and vegetables. The sailors' healthy diet and clean living conditions kept scurvy away. But the crew got another disease called malaria. Mosquitos spread this deadly disease. Malaria causes fever and chills. About one-third of Cook's crew died from malaria.

Cook sailed across the Indian Ocean and around the Cape of Good Hope. His remaining crew recovered from illness. On July 13, 1771, he and his crew arrived back in England.

Chapter 3

Sailing around the World Alone

In 1898, Joshua Slocum became the first person to sail around the world alone. He traveled more than 46,000 miles (74,000 kilometers) in a sloop named the *Spray*. His adventure took more than three years to complete.

Challenges

The *Spray* was an old boat in need of repair. Slocum spent 13 months rebuilding the *Spray*. He set sail on April 24, 1895, from Boston, Massachusetts. He sailed east across the Atlantic Ocean.

Slocum quickly discovered that loneliness would become a great challenge. Early in his

Joshua Slocum was the first person to sail around the world alone.

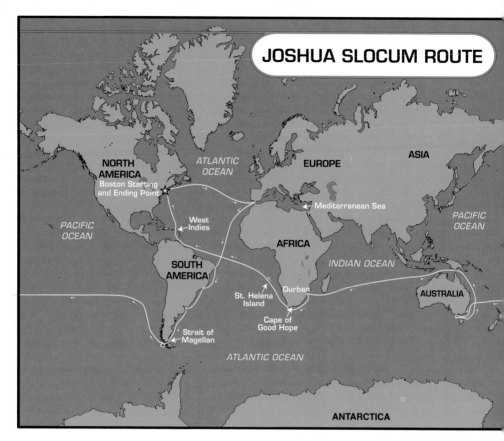

adventure, he encountered thick fog. The fog made him feel even more alone. He tried talking to himself, to his boat, or to the moon. But his speaking voice sounded strange to him. Instead, he sang songs to entertain himself.

One day, Slocum got sick from some food that he ate. He was in pain and felt weak and tired. He saw that a huge storm was near. He lay down on the cabin floor. He was too sick to guide the ship. He began to hallucinate. He saw things that were not really there. Slocum thought that he saw someone steering the boat. The figure told him that he would guide the *Spray* so that Slocum could rest and recover. Slocum felt better after the storm passed. He found that the boat was still following his planned course.

A Change of Plans
Slocum originally planned to sail across the Mediterranean Sea to the Suez Canal. This canal in Egypt connects the Mediterranean Sea and the Red Sea. British Navy officers warned Slocum about pirates in this area. Slocum then decided to turn around and sail west around the world.

Slocum headed across the Atlantic Ocean again. This time, he traveled toward Brazil. He continued south around South America.

Slocum then sailed to the Strait of Magellan. Constant wind and storms there made sailing very dangerous. He made it through the strait. But a storm pushed him back east. He carefully navigated the dangerous waters. He had to sail through the Strait of Magellan once again. It took him about two months to sail through this area.

Slocum rebuilt his boat *Spray* for his journey.

The Pacific and Indian Oceans

Slocum finally reached the Pacific Ocean. He spent 72 days crossing the Pacific. He was still lonely at times. But he passed the time reading books and relaxing.

Slocum reached the Samoa Islands. He visited with people and enjoyed the beauty of the islands. He then traveled to Sydney, Australia. He met people and explored

Australia's coast. He then sailed into the
Indian Ocean toward Africa.

Slocum sailed to Durban, South Africa.
He spent about one month there. He bought
new books and visited with people.

The Last Leg

Slocum stopped at St. Helena Island in the
southern Atlantic Ocean on his way north to
the West Indies. There, he brought a goat on
board for companionship. Slocum later called
this goat the worst pirate he met on his entire
voyage. The goat ate some of his rope, sails,
and his map of the West Indies. The goat also
ate Slocum's straw hat. At his next stop,
Slocum left the goat on shore.

After three years, Slocum returned to the
eastern coast of the United States. He sailed
into Fairhaven, Massachusetts, on July 3, 1898.
He had sailed around the world alone.

Slocum was famous when he returned
home. He spoke and wrote about his travels. In
1909, Slocum set sail on the *Spray* from
Bristol, Rhode Island. He traveled toward
South America. He was never seen again.

Chapter 4

More Challenges

Sailors continue to seek adventure and set new records. Some sailors hope to be the fastest, the youngest, or the oldest to set new sailing records.

Robin Lee Graham

Robin Lee Graham learned to sail at a young age. Graham's father taught him how to check and repair his boat and equipment. Graham also learned how to predict the actions of the wind and the sea.

When he was 16 years old, Graham told his parents that he wanted to sail alone around the world. His parents understood his desire to be at sea. In 1962 and 1963, the family had spent

Robin Lee Graham became the youngest person to sail alone around the world.

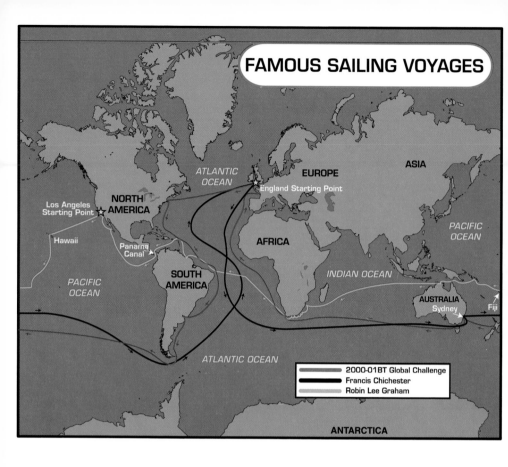

more than a year at sea. On July 27, 1965, Graham began his journey from Los Angeles, California. He sailed toward Hawaii in his 24-foot (7.3-meter) sloop called the *Dove*.

Graham spent nearly five years sailing around the world. He visited many cities and towns along the way. Graham survived severe weather, a collapsed mast, and being tossed overboard. Loneliness was his greatest challenge. But he also enjoyed the freedom of the open sea.

In 1966, Graham met Patti Ratterree during a stop in Fiji. They fell in love and married. Patti followed Graham's route on land so that they could meet at his stops.

Graham returned to Los Angeles on April 30, 1970. He became the youngest solo circumnavigator. He was 21 years old at the end of his 30,600-mile (49,200-kilometer) journey.

Francis Chichester

In 1967, Francis Chichester became the first person to sail around the world with only one stop. He was 64 years old at the time of his journey. He sailed in a 53-foot (16-meter) ketch called the *Gipsy Moth IV*. The trip consisted of two legs. The first leg took him from England to Sydney, Australia. The second leg took him back to England.

Chichester faced a major problem before reaching Australia. His self-steering gear broke. This gear kept the boat on course while Chichester was free to move about the boat. Without the self-steering gear, he had to steer the boat himself at all times. He had to fix the problem. Chichester set the ropes and sails to steer the boat automatically. He arrived in Australia after 107 days at sea.

Many people tried to convince Chichester to stop his travels. In Sydney, he looked tired and worn out. But Chichester ignored them. He wanted to prove to himself that he could complete this challenge. He concentrated on getting his boat ready for the next leg. He patched leaks and repaired the self-steering gear. He tried to regain his strength and get plenty of rest. He spent about five weeks in Australia before he again set sail.

Chichester faced a severe storm during his first night at sea. The boat withstood great damage. Chichester spent the next few weeks making repairs. He felt weak and afraid. But

Francis Chichester made only one stop on his around-the-world voyage.

Chay Blyth sailed around the world alone without stopping.

he made it back to England after 274 days. This time included 226 days of sailing. He had successfully sailed around the world.

Chay Blyth

In August 1971, Chay Blyth set a new record. He sailed around the world without stopping. He sailed from east to west. This direction is against the prevailing winds.

It is more difficult to sail in this direction. This expedition took Blyth almost 300 days. He sailed in a ketch called the *British Steel*.

Chay Blyth currently runs the BT Global Challenge. In this race, people without much offshore racing experience learn to sail ocean racing boats. The people are divided into crews. An experienced captain leads these amateur crews on a race around the world. The race follows the same route against the prevailing winds that Blyth took in 1971. The race takes an average of 10 months to complete.

Chapter 5

Sailing Today

Sailors have discovered new lands and circled the globe. But challenges still remain. Some sailors attempt new and difficult routes that no one has ever sailed. Others try to set speed records. Many sailing races challenge sailors to be in top physical and mental condition.

Around Alone
Sailors race alone around the world in an event called Around Alone. The race first took place in 1982 under the name BOC Challenge. It takes place once every four years.

Around Alone covers more distance than any other race in the world. It covers about 27,000 miles (43,000 kilometers). Sailors take

Sailors race alone around the world in an event called Around Alone.

Catherine Chabaud was the first woman to sail alone around the world nonstop.

an average of 150 days to complete the race. Throughout the race, sailors are allowed to stop at ports for repairs to their boats.

Philippe Jeantot won the first BOC Challenge. He set a new solo circumnavigation record with a time of 159 days, 2 hours, and 26 minutes. Jeantot won the race again in 1987. He beat his previous record with a time of 134 days, 5 hours, and 24 minutes.

During the 1987 race, Jeantot kept to a strict schedule. He slept no more than an hour at one time and no more than five hours in a day. He used a computerized alarm system to wake himself up. A horn wailed if the boat's speed or the wind's direction changed.

The Vendée Globe
In 1989, Jeantot organized a race called the Vendée Globe. Jeantot took part and finished fourth in the race. He finished in 113 days, 23 hours, and 47 minutes. Frenchman Titouan Lamazou won the race in 109 days, 8 hours, and 49 minutes. The race takes place every three to four years. Each sailor travels alone nonstop around the world. The French Federation of Sailing must approve each competitor.

Catherine Chabaud competed in the 1996–97 Vendée Globe. During this race, she became the first female sailor to circumnavigate the world alone nonstop. Chabaud completed the Vendée Globe in 140 days. She finished in sixth place.

During the race, Chabaud slept only 10 minutes to 3 hours at a time. She had to get up often to check her equipment.

At one point, Chabaud's boat half-capsized. Her mast was in the water. She did not panic. She got the boat upright and finished the race.

Sailors set two important records in the 2000–01 Vendée Globe. Michel Desjoyeaux won the race in 93 days, 3 hours, and 57 minutes. This time is the record for the fastest solo nonstop circumnavigation.

Ellen MacArthur finished the race in second place. She completed the race in 94 days, 4 hours, and 25 minutes. This time set a record for a female sailor completing a solo nonstop circumnavigation. MacArthur was just 24 years old at the time.

Sailing adventures are a test of emotions as well as a test of skills. Sailors must deal with being lonely and tired. They must keep calm when storms arise. But new sailors continue to enjoy these challenges.

In 2001, Ellen MacArthur completed the fastest solo nonstop circumnavigation by a woman.

TIMELINE

| 1500s–1700s | 1800s–1900s | 1980s–1990s | 2000s |

1519–1522
Crew led by Ferdinand Magellan completes the first circumnavigation.

1577–1580
Sir Francis Drake leads a crew on the second circumnavigation.

1768–1771
James Cook leads a crew around the world while making new detailed maps of the Pacific Ocean.

1895–1898
Joshua Slocum sails alone around the world. He is the first sailor to ever do this.

1965–1970
Robin Lee Graham becomes the youngest person to sail alone around the world. He was 21 years old when he completed his voyage.

1966–1967
Francis Chichester sails alone around the world while stopping only once.

1970–1971
Chay Blyth sails alone around the world without stopping.

1980s
Global positioning system is developed.

1982
The first Around Alone race takes place. It is called the BOC Challenge at this time.

1989
Philippe Jeantot organizes the first Vendée Globe race. He finishes the race in fourth place.

1996
At age 18, David Dicks becomes the youngest person to sail alone around the world.

1996–1997
Catherine Chabaud becomes the first woman to sail alone around the world nonstop.

2000–2001
Michel Desjoyea wins the Vendée Globe. He sets th record for the fastest solo circumnavigatio

2000–2001
Ellen MacArthur finishes second i the Vendée Glob She sets the record for the fastest solo circumnavigatio by a woman.

Words to Know

circumnavigate (sur-kuhm-NAV-uh-gate)—to sail or travel completely around the world

expedition (ek-spuh-DISH-uhn)—a long journey made for a special purpose

fleet (FLEET)—a group of ships that sail together

headsail (HED-sayl)—the sail that is located in front of the main mast

mainsail (MAYN-sayl)—the sail that is located behind the main mast

scurvy (SKUR-vee)—a disease caused by a lack of vitamin C; scurvy causes bleeding gums and weakness.

strait (STRAYT)—a narrow strip of water that connects two larger bodies of water

To Learn More

Gallagher, Jim. *Ferdinand Magellan and the First Voyage around the World.* Explorers of New Worlds. Philadelphia: Chelsea House, 2000.

Gallagher, Jim. *Sir Francis Drake and the Start of a World Empire.* Explorers of New Worlds. Philadelphia: Chelsea House, 2000.

Lasky, Kathryn. *Born in the Breezes: The Voyages of Joshua Slocum.* New York: Orchard Books, 2001.

Meltzer, Milton. *Captain James Cook.* Great Explorations. New York: Benchmark Books, 2001.

Otfinoski, Steven. *Into the Wind: Sailboats Then and Now.* Here We Go! Tarrytown, N.Y.: Benchmark Books, 1997.

Useful Addresses

Canadian Yachting Association
Portsmouth Olympic Harbour
53 Yonge Street
Kingston, ON K7M 6G4
Canada

Joshua Slocum Society International
15 Codfish Hill Road Extension
Bethel, CT 06801

United States Sailing Association
P.O. Box 1260
15 Maritime Drive
Portsmouth, RI 02871-0907

Internet Sites

BT Global Challenge
http://www.btchallenge.com

Canadian Yachting Association
http://www.sailing.ca

Joshua Slocum Society International
http://www.mcallen.lib.tx.us/orgs/
    SLOCUM.HTM

Sailnet
http://www.sailnet.com

United States Sailing Association
http://www.ussailing.org

Index